Max Learns
THE IMPORTANCE OF PRACTICE

Cory Lemay

Illustrated by Kseniya Bratukhina

Max Learns the Importance of Practice by Cory Lemay
First edition 2021.

Author E-Mail: CoryLemayBooks@gmail.com

Illustrated by Kseniya Bratukhina

ISBN: 978-0-578-32424-1

To my students - who inspire me everyday to keep learning and growing.

Max always had a dream!

His vision was to paint.

But his paintings were just no good.

Friends would say "We love it!",
then faint.

But he never asked for help.
And he never tried to learn.
"An artist," Max said,
"Knows already on his own."

"You see, a painter never needs to learn!
Art's a skill you're given when you're born."

Every few days, Max would explore his local museum.
"Wow! Look at that! The paintings are great!"
How he just loved to see them!

Max wished he could draw like his idols.
But he was sure he never could.
"Nothing I make, could ever be THAT good."

"Now wait!" Max thought.

"If I put these paintings up on my walls at home. My friends would think I made them all on my own."

"I'd be the greatest artist my friends have ever known!"

"So alright," Max said, "This is the deal."
"All I need to do is go in and steal!"

"Besides, if I take them, the artists won't mind.
In five or ten minutes, they'll make new ones just
fine!"

Max's paws only briefly touched the frame.
But the passerby's reaction was surprise just the same!

"What are you doing?" called out the man with a scream.
Max said, "I work here you see, it's time these frames get cleaned!"

"Now, help me give this a lift.
It's alright! I insist!"

Max thought, "My plan is working so far!"
As the passerby helped Max load it into his car.

Max stared with joy at his pile of prizes.
"There are so many paintings of so many sizes!"

Max wondered about the walls he left bare.
"I bet there are great new paintings up there!
Give the artist ten minutes, he wouldn't even
care!"

What Max did now find, was quite a surprise.
The artist did mind. He minded BIG TIME!

The painter sat on the floor, dripping and sobbing.
There were so many tears, the floor needed mopping!

Max asked him, "Why are you sad? What's with these tears?"

"Well Max, you see, painting this took me years!"

"A beautiful painting takes time to create.
Your first try, I've found, is never that great."

"It takes time to improve what you're doing, you
see.
That's true for you, and oh boy, that's true for
me!"

Max could see now, how he hurt with his crime.
"Making great art, clearly takes time!"

"You can't steal hard work, because you'll never improve.
If you try to fake it, you'll just look like you do."

So Max gave the art back and said he was sorry
From the beginning to end, he shared his whole story.

The artist explained,
"When I was your age, I felt just the same.
For quite a while, my paintings were lame.
So come back here at the end of the day,
And I'll teach you to paint in the most beautiful
way!"

So the artist taught Max how to paint a beautiful
canvas.
And Max learned all he needed was a little
practice.

Made in the USA
Las Vegas, NV
23 November 2021

35170133R00019